This book belongs to

_____

Old Bear

Scribblers

IT wasn't anybody's birthday, but Bramwell Brown had a feeling that today was going to be a special day. He was sitting thoughtfully on the windowsill with his friends Duck, Rabbit and Little Bear when he suddenly remembered that someone wasn't there who should be.

A VERY long time ago, he had
seen his good friend Old Bear being packed
away in a box. Then he was taken up
a ladder, through a trap door and into
the attic. The children were being
too rough with him and he
needed somewhere safe
to go for a while.

'HAS he been forgotten, do you think?' Bramwell asked his friends.

'I think he might have been,' said Rabbit.

'Well,' said Little Bear, 'isn't it time he came back down with us? The children are older now and would look after him properly. Let's go and get him!'

'What a marvellous idea!' said Bramwell. 'But how can we rescue him? It's a long way up to the attic and we haven't got a ladder.'

'We could build a tower of bricks,' suggested Little Bear.

Rabbit collected all the bricks and the others set about building the tower. It grew very tall, and Little Bear was just putting on the last brick when the tower began to wobble.

'Look out!' he cried as the whole thing came tumbling down.

CRASH!

'Never mind,' said Bramwell, helping Little Bear to his feet. 'We'll just have to think of something else.'

'L ET'S try making *ourselves* into a tower,' said Duck.

'Good idea!' said Bramwell.

Little Bear climbed on top of Rabbit's head and Rabbit hopped onto Duck's beak. They stretched up as far as they could, but then Duck opened his beak to say something, Rabbit wobbled, and they all collapsed on top of Bramwell.

'Sorry,' said Duck, 'perhaps that wasn't a very good idea.'

'Not one of your best,' replied Bramwell from somewhere underneath the heap.

'I KNOW!' said Rabbit. 'Let's try bouncing on the bed.'

'Trust you to think of that,' said Bramwell. 'You never can resist a bit of bouncing, especially when it's not allowed.'

Rabbit climbed onto the bed and began to bounce

up and down,

up and down,

up and down.

The others joined him. They bounced higher and higher but *still* they couldn't reach the trap door in the ceiling.

DUCK began to cry. 'Oh dear,' he sobbed.
  'What are we going to do now? We'll never be able to
rescue Old Bear and he'll be stuck up there getting lonelier
and lonelier for ever and ever.'
  'We mustn't give up,' said Bramwell firmly.
'Come on Little Bear, you're good at ideas.'

But Little Bear had already noticed
the plant in the corner of the room.

'I'VE got it!' he cried. 'I could climb up this plant, swing from the leaves, kick the trap door open and jump in!'

In case it wobbled, Bramwell Brown, Duck and Rabbit steadied the pot. Little Bear bravely climbed up the plant until he reached the very top leaf. He took hold of it and started to swing to and fro, but he swung so hard that the leaf broke . . . SNAP!

He came crashing down. Luckily, Bramwell Brown was right underneath to catch him in his paws.

'That was a rotten idea,' said Little Bear.

'What I was thinking,' said Duck, 'was that it is a pity I can't fly very well, as I could have been quite a help.'

'Ah ha!' said Bramwell. 'That, my dear Duck, has given me a very good idea. I really think this one might work.'

IN the corner of the playroom was a little wooden plane with a propeller that went round and round.

'We could use this plane to get to the trap door,' said Bramwell. 'Rather dangerous, I know, but quite honestly I can't bear to think of Old Bear up there alone for a minute longer.'

'I'll be pilot,' said Rabbit, hopping up and down, making plane noises.

'And I'll stand on the back and push the trap door open with my paintbrush,' said Little Bear.

'But how will you get down?' asked Duck.

'I've already thought of that,' said Bramwell. 'They can use these handkerchiefs as parachutes and we'll catch them in a blanket.'

BRAMWELL gave Little Bear two big
handkerchiefs and a torch so he could see into the attic.
Then he began to wind up the propeller of the plane.
 Rabbit and Little Bear climbed aboard and Bramwell
began the countdown:

'Five,

Four,

Three,

Two,

One,

GO!'

They were off! The plane whizzed along
the carpet and flew up into the air.

THE little plane flew beautifully and the first time they passed the trap door Little Bear was able to push the lid open with his paintbrush. Then Rabbit circled the plane again, this time very close to the hole. Little Bear grabbed the edge and with a mighty heave he pulled himself inside.

He got out his torch and looked around. The attic was very dark and quiet: full of boxes, old clothes and dust. He couldn't see Old Bear at all.

'Any bears in here?' he whispered, and stood still to listen. From somewhere quite near he heard a muffled Grrrrrrr followed by 'Did somebody say something?'

Little Bear moved a few things aside and there, propped up against a cardboard box and covered in dust, was Old Bear.

L ITTLE Bear jumped up
and down with excitement.

'Old Bear!

Old Bear!

I've found Old Bear!'

'So you have,' said Old Bear.

'Have you been lonely?' asked Little Bear.

'Quite lonely,' said Old Bear. 'But I've been asleep a lot of
the time.'

'Well,' said Little Bear kindly, 'would you like to come
back to the playroom with us now?'

'That would be lovely,' replied Old Bear. 'But how will we
get down?'

'Don't worry about that,' said Little Bear, 'Bramwell has
thought of everything. He's given us these handkerchiefs to
use as parachutes.'

'GOOD old Bramwell,' said the old teddy. 'I'm glad
he didn't forget me.'

Old Bear stood up and shook the dust out of his fur and
Little Bear helped him into his parachute. They went over
to the hole in the ceiling.

'Ready,' shouted Rabbit.

'Steady,' shouted Duck.

'GO!' shouted Bramwell Brown.

The two bears leapt bravely from the hole in the ceiling.
Their handkerchief parachutes opened out and they
floated gently down . . . landing safely in the blanket.

'WELCOME home, Old Bear,' said Bramwell Brown, patting his friend on the back. The others patted him too, just to make him feel at home.

'It's nice to have you back,' they said.
'It's nice to be back,' replied Old Bear.

THAT night, when all the animals were tucked up in bed, Bramwell thought about the day's adventures and looked at the others.

Rabbit was dreaming exciting dreams about bouncing as high as an aeroplane.

Duck was dreaming that he could really fly and was rescuing bears from all sorts of high places.

Little Bear was dreaming of all the interesting things he had seen in the attic, and Old Bear was dreaming about the good times he would have now he was back with his friends.

'Hmm,' said Bramwell, happily, 'I knew it was going to be a special day.'

Turn the page to find out more in
the Old Bear scrapbook...

About Jane Hissey

Original rough sketches for *Old Bear*

Jane has always loved writing and drawing. Throughout much of her childhood she lived in Norfolk and wandered the fields and lanes with pencil and sketchbook.

She studied illustration and design in Brighton, where she met her husband, Ivan, who is also an illustrator. After college, they settled in Sussex and Jane taught art for a few years before leaving to have her first child, Owen. Since then she has had two more children; Alison and Ralph, and has written and illustrated over 20 picture books.

Jane working in her studio

She prepares a dummy book of rough sketches before she begins the finished drawings. For these she draws first in pencil then, using coloured pencils, she builds up layers of colour, adding details towards the end. Each drawing takes many, many hours and a whole book can take a year.

About Old Bear

Jane (aged 3) taking Old Bear for a picnic

When Jane started writing and illustrating she chose Old Bear to be the star of her first book. He was soon joined by other family toys: Bramwell Brown, Little Bear, Rabbit and Duck. Since then Old Bear has travelled everywhere with Jane, visiting schools, libraries and book fairs. He has met thousands of children who have read about his adventures and Jane has drawn him so many times she has lost count!

Jane (aged 3), her brother Nigel and Old Bear

Old Bear is a real teddy bear. He was given to Jane, when she was a baby, by her grandmother. Of course he wasn't an old bear then, he was brand new! Throughout her childhood, he was Jane's favourite teddy and he joined in all her games. When his nose became worn or an eye became wobbly, Jane's mother would stitch him a new one. When the family moved abroad for a while, Old Bear really was packed away in the attic, though his rescue was not quite as dramatic as in the Old Bear story.

The original Old Bear toys

Old Bear around the world

Jane's Old Bear books have been translated into lots of different languages and have been read by children all over the world. Jane has hand-written replies to thousands of letters from young readers and their parents, eager to know more about Old Bear and his friends. Some have even been writing to Jane for over twenty years!

Old Bear Front Covers

German

Korean

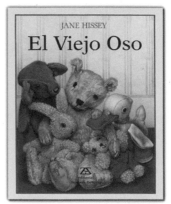

Spanish

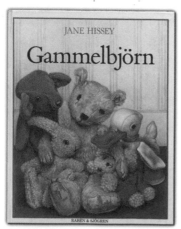

Swedish

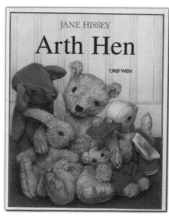

Welsh

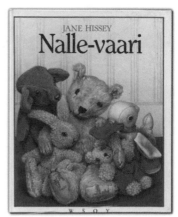

Finnish

Old Bear on screen

Following the success of the books, it wasn't long before Jane was asked to write a TV series for the toys. Model animation was chosen and sets were built to look just like the drawings in the books. Each ten-minute episode took about five weeks to film and Old Bear Stories won many awards including a BAFTA. Forty episodes were produced and seen in 90 different countries.

Jane signing books

The Old Bear animation models celebrating their award!

The books and TV inspired a huge range of merchandising and soon you could buy Old Bear stationery, mugs, calendars, alarm clocks, bubble bath and baby clothes. You could even have your own Old Bear toy!

Royal Doulton figures based on Old Bear characters

For Owen, Alison and Ralph

SALARIYA

www.salariya.com

This edition published in Great Britain in MMXIII by Scribblers, a division of Book House,
an imprint of The Salariya Book Company Ltd
25 Marlborough Place,
Brighton BN1 1UB

www.scribblersbooks.com
www.janehissey.co.uk

First published in Great Britain in MCMLXXXVI by Hutchinson Children's Books

ISBN-13: 978-1-908177-82-7

1 3 5 7 9 8 6 4 2

A CIP catalogue record for this book is available from the British Library.

Printed and bound in China
Printed on paper from sustainable sources

shop online

shop.salariya.com